Magic Animal Café

Published by Sweet Cherry Publishing Limited
Unit 36, Vulcan House,
Vulcan Road,
Leicester, LE5 3EF
United Kingdom

First published in the UK in 2022
2022 edition

2 4 6 8 10 9 7 5 3 1

ISBN: 978-1-78226-931-1

Magic Animal Café: Shazza the Homesick Cockatoo

Cover design by Fabiana Attanasio and Jessica Walters
Illustrations by Fabiana Attanasio

www.sweetcherrypublishing.com

Printed and bound in the India
I.TP002

Magic Animal Café
Shazza
the Homesick
Cockatoo

Stella Tarakson

Illustrated by
Fabiana Attanasio

Chapter One

'Where do you want the espresso machine?' asked a man in overalls, hefting a large box.

'On that counter, over to the left.' Ellie's mum rubbed her hands together, looking pleased. 'It's really happening,' she said. 'Soon we'll be ready to open!'

Ellie hadn't seen her mum look so happy in years. Even yesterday's

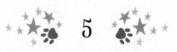

worrying news hadn't upset her. Ellie had overheard a man planning to build something across the road that would have other coffee shops inside it. They would be clean and modern, unlike Mum's café, which was on the ground floor of a tired old building. The man had gone on to say that when Mum's café flopped, he would buy it from her at a low price.

Ellie's mum had refused to be frightened. 'I'm not going to be bullied by developers,' she'd insisted. 'People will come to us because we're different – there are no other cat cafés around! Cattucino will do well, you'll see.'

Ellie was glad Mum was so confident but wished she'd take the threat more seriously. At least she could try to find out more about it. Ellie and her new friend Blake couldn't help feeling worried.

'Why don't they have dog cafés, too?' Blake asked, holding his wriggling Labrador puppy against his chest. Blake and his parents had moved into the second floor flat above the café, while Ellie and her mum lived on the first floor. They'd moved to England from Australia to set up an animal rescue centre.

Ellie rolled her eyes at Blake's question. 'Maybe it's because people don't like getting slobbered over.'

Ellie had never been much of a dog person. Cats were calmer, quieter and neater – Ellie and her mum owned eight of them. They were all going to be part of the new café. But she had to admit that she was starting to like Choccy, who was rather sweet. She ruffled the puppy's ears and he wagged his tail.

'See, Ellie?' Choccy said, his tail thumping against Blake. 'No licking.'

'That's right. You're a fast learner–' Ellie started to say, before Blake flashed her a warning look. Ellie clamped her mouth shut. She checked to see whether Mum had noticed, but she was busy watching the men putting the espresso machine in place.

Ellie and Blake had an agreement. For the time being at least, they weren't going to tell anybody that they could talk to animals. It was more fun to keep it to themselves.

Ellie and Blake weren't sure exactly how, but their exciting new ability had something to do with an old-fashioned telephone they'd found. The magic started just after the children rang the faded numbers written on a piece of paper in the centre of the dial.

'Scuse me, careful now.'

Something hard bumped against
Ellie's back. She stepped backwards

as a man carrying a rug pushed past her, straight into the path of two others who were moving a table.

'Why don't you two go out for a bit?' Mum suggested, pointing out the spot where she wanted the table placed. 'Have some fun before school starts. There's a park across the road. You could take your sketch pad and do a drawing for me.'

Ellie and Blake exchanged a look. Yesterday the man had said the new development would be across the road.

Ellie grabbed her sketching set, Blake clipped on Choccy's lead, and they were out the door.

'Let's see if we find out what's going on,' Blake said.

'Exactly what I was thinking,' Ellie agreed. 'But how?'

 12

'I'm not sure. There might be some signs up around the park.'

As they waited for the traffic lights to change, Ellie had a thought. 'Hey, do you think we can talk to animals out here too? Or just at home where the phone is?'

'Choccy?' Blake said, looking down at the puppy pulling on the lead. 'Can you still understand us?'

'Walkies walkies walkies walkies!' The excited chant was all they could get out of Choccy just then, but it was enough for Blake. He grinned at Ellie as if to say: 'There's your answer.'

'But do you think the magic only works between us?' Ellie said.

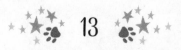

'Between you, me, Choccy, the cats and the mice?'

'Let's see while we're out,' Blake suggested. 'We'll try talking to some other animals.'

Ellie nodded in agreement and secretly crossed her fingers.

They walked through the park and looked for signs announcing new building work. At the same time, they kept an eye out for animals to talk to. It wasn't easy. There were plenty of dogs about, but they were all under the close watch of their owners. Birds flew past, but the children didn't want to attract attention by calling out to them. A squirrel looked at them curiously but was chased off by Choccy.

'No signs or notices at all,' Ellie said, after they'd walked around the whole park.

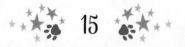

Blake shrugged. 'Maybe we should go around again, in case we missed anything.'

'You can, if you like. I want to do a quick sketch for Mum.' Ellie sat on a wooden bench underneath a large oak tree.

'All right. Coming, Choccy?'

The little brown Labrador spun in a circle. 'Am gonna run fast!' he barked. Then he bounded off, leaving Blake to catch up.

'Wish me luck!' Blake called to Ellie as he started running.

Ellie waved after them, then opened her sketch pad. She saw the drawing she'd made of her old house and quickly turned to a fresh page. It was over two weeks since Ellie had moved out of her old, familiar home, and she was still homesick. But meeting Blake and being able to talk to animals had given her lots of other things to think about.

If only she didn't have to go to a new school and try to make new friends – but that was a whole week away, she reminded herself. Until then, she would have fun testing out her new talking-to-animals skills.

She looked around for something to draw and picked out some late roses – her mum's favourite flower.

Pursing her lips in concentration,
Ellie had just started to sketch out
the long stems when –

'*Aairrk!*'

– something large, white
and noisy shot out of the
oak tree straight towards
her face.

Chapter Two

'Gah!' Ellie ducked as an odd-looking creature zoomed right over her head, ruffling her hair as it passed. It looked like a bird – a very large one. It had a glossy blue and yellow rectangle for a head.

'What was that?' Ellie breathed, sitting up again.

'Aairrk!'

Whatever it was, it was coming back.
Ellie threw up her hands to protect her face
and ducked again. She felt a puff of air

and heard wings beating near her head.

'Get it off!' an angry voice squawked in her ear.

'Get what off?' Ellie opened a gap between her fingers and peered through. It was definitely some sort of bird. She was talking to a bird!

'What do you think?' it answered crossly, coming to perch on the bench next to her. Its voice was muffled. 'There's something on my head. Get it off!'

Ellie shook off her astonishment. 'Oh! I see.'

The blue and yellow rectangle was an empty crisp packet. Or rather, it was empty except for the bird's head.

'Sit still,' she said. Feeling slightly nervous – after all, it was a very big bird, and it had very powerful-looking claws – Ellie reached over and pinched a corner of the crisp packet. She gave a gentle tug and off it came.

'Finally!' the bird squawked, raising its crest of bright yellow feathers. Ellie thought it looked like a mohawk and she had to stop herself from giggling. The bird fixed her with its bright, red-black eyes and cocked its head. 'What's so funny?'

'Nothing,' she reassured it. 'Except you were wearing a crisp packet.'

'Is that what it was?' The bird pecked at the bag. 'I was looking for numnums.'

'What are numnums?'

'My favourite food, of course! I thought there might be some in there.'

It plucked the packet out of Ellie's hand and threw it at her feet. 'But it was empty. Have you got anything I can eat?'

'No, sorry.'

The bird looked at the sketch pad on Ellie's lap. 'How about that?'

'That's not food. It's a book for drawing pictures in.'

'I bet I could pick it up, carry it away and drop it on someone's head!'

Ellie gaped at the bird. 'I'm sure you could, but they might not like that.'

'Aairrk! But I would. I'd also like to sharpen my beak by chomping on that bench.'

Ellie eyed the solid wood bench. 'Don't do that,' she said. 'You might break your beak.'

'I might break the bench!' The bird gave the wooden slat it was sitting on a vicious jab with its beak.

'Um, okay ...' Ellie bit her lip, torn between wonder and confusion. She was thrilled to be able to talk to the bird, but wasn't sure how to make sense of what it was saying back. Above all, she

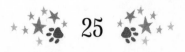

wanted to share her discovery with someone else.

'Blake!' she cried, when she saw a familiar figure returning.

'There are definitely no signs up,' Blake said as he drew nearer. 'Maybe there's someone-' He stopped in his tracks when he saw the bird. 'A sulphur-crested cockatoo! I haven't seen one of those since we left Sydney.' He scooped Choccy up in his arms so that he wouldn't be able to chase the bird away.

Ellie moved along the bench to make room. 'We've been talking to each other!' she said excitedly. 'That

means the magic works with other animals too, right? It's not just the ones who've been around the phone!'

'I dunno. There are lots of talking cockatoos. Their owners teach them how to do it.' Blake sat next to the bird. 'Who's a pretty boy, then? Polly want a cracker?'

The bird snapped its beak. 'I'm a girl, not a boy! And my name's not Polly. It's Shazza. But you may feed me a cracker anyway.' Shazza opened her beak wide, showing her stubby dark tongue.

Blake blinked, obviously as surprised as Ellie had been. 'I'm sorry, I don't have any.'

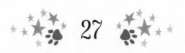

'Then why did you offer me one?'

Blake grinned at Ellie. 'You're right. This bird's definitely talking to us, not just copying what we say. But how did she get here? They don't live in this country, as far as I know.' He turned to the bird. 'What are you doing in England, Shazza?'

Shazza tilted her head to the side. 'What's England? Is it yummy? Can I eat it?'

'No, it's a place. How did you get here? Are you an escaped pet?'

'Aairrk! Mine is a tragic story. A very long, very sad story.' Shazza fluffed out her feathers dramatically. 'Do you want to hear it?'

'No!' barked Choccy, wriggling against Blake's chest. 'I want to play.'

'Ssh, Choccy. If you're quiet, I'll give you a treat.'

'Treat!'

Blake handed his puppy a rawhide chew, and Choccy settled on the grass to gnaw at it.

'Is that my numnums?' Shazza asked, looking at the dried animal skin. She swooped down and pecked at it before Choccy could pull it away.

'Blech, no!' Shazza spat. 'He can keep it!' Shazza hopped back onto the bench. 'Anyway, you're right, I used to be a pet. I had the best

human ever. One who gave me numnums every day.'

'What happened?' Ellie asked, sensing a 'but'.

'My human got old. We cockatoos live a long time, you know. And she was already in her seventies when she adopted me.' Shazza's crest flopped down as she spoke. 'She got sick. One day, she left and didn't come back. I remember her family came over and started taking things out of our house. They stuck me in a cage. I hate cages! My human always let me fly free. They kept saying "what do we do about the bird?" and things like that.'

Ellie shifted uncomfortably in her seat. She could see where this was going.

'I learnt to undo the latch on the cage. Every time they locked me up, I escaped. Eventually they threw me out,' Shazza said grimly. '"Letting me go", they called it. They said I'd be fine. I'd have no trouble finding food. I could just join "the wild ones".' Shazza cocked her head. 'Have you ever tried living with a bunch of wild cockatoos? It's not easy.'

'But Shazza,' Blake said, confused, 'there are no wild cockatoos in England.'

'Don't I know it! There are thousands where I come from. They were difficult, but they were family. I don't have any family here. I don't even have any friends. I'm sooooo lonely!' she wailed.

Blake petted Shazza soothingly. 'There, there,' he said.

'We'll be your friends,' Ellie added.

Shazza looked at them with eyes that had suddenly lost their sadness. 'You mean you'll help me?'

'Of course we will!' Ellie said immediately.

Blake was more cautious. 'Help you how, exactly?'

'Help me get back home, of course.'

Chapter Three

'But I still don't understand,' said Ellie. 'Where is home?' Blake was right; cockatoos didn't exist in the wild in England.

'I don't know where,' Shazza admitted, 'but it's different from here.' The bird looked at the cloudy sky and shivered. 'Back home there was sunshine, huge open spaces and all the balconies I could eat. I miss it.'

Blake was nodding knowingly. 'Definitely Australia.' He shielded his mouth with his hand and added in a lower voice to Ellie, 'Cockatoos are native back home, and they're real pests. They destroy everything. They chew through phone cables. They break open streetlamp covers and swing on them. If you start feeding cockatoos on your balcony or in your garden and then stop, they'll eat your woodwork instead. I've even seen them pluck washing off clothes lines and fly away with it.'

Ellie was shocked. She'd never seen birds behave like that before!

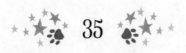

'What's that? What are you saying?' Shazza jerked her head towards Blake.

'Nothing. Just that you came from

the same place I did.' For a moment
Blake looked sad, then his face
cleared. 'But how did you get here?'
he asked. 'It's a very long way.'

'How did you get here?' Shazza replied.

Blake shrugged. 'We flew.'

'Aairrk!' Shazza tilted her head one way and then another. 'Where are your wings?'

'Not that sort of flying, silly. I meant in an aeroplane. Like that one.' He pointed to the sky where a small dot was leaving a long white trail as a jet flew overhead.

Shazza fluffed up her feathers and looked offended. 'No need to be rude. Maybe that's how I got here too.'

'That's not poss–' Blake started, but Ellie held up her hand.

'What makes you say that?' she asked.

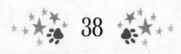

'Well, when I was kicked out of my home, I went to live with my wild brothers and sisters. At first, they didn't want me to join their flock, but I hung around anyway.'

Ellie nodded. 'It's not easy breaking into groups,' she said, thinking of the new school year ahead.

'Even when they agreed to let me stay,' Shazza continued, 'life wasn't great. They didn't know anything about numnums. I had to eat what they ate: seeds and berries and leaf buds – blech.'

'Blech,' Choccy echoed, raising his head. Blake patted him to keep him quiet.

'I decided to go hunting for proper food,' Shazza continued. 'Each day

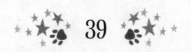

I went further and further until I
smelt numnums. It was coming from
a human, so I followed him into
something that looked like a big metal
shed. Inside it was full of animals in

crates and cages. I think the human left
because there was a bang and everything
went dark. After a while, I felt myself
rising up, up, up without using my
wings, and there was a terrible noise.

I was scared – all the animals were
– but eventually I fell asleep. When I
woke up, the door was open. I tried
to fly out, but humans caught me
and put me in a cage like the rest of
the animals. We were moved into
another shed. The next time they
opened the door, I escaped my cage
and flew away. That's how I got here.'

  After a moment, Ellie said, 'I think
I get it. You must've got stuck in
the animal hold of an aeroplane.
The staff probably thought you'd
escaped your cage so they put you
in one.' She looked at Blake. 'What
do we do? How do we get her back
to Australia?'

Blake raked a hand through his hair. 'I have no idea. It's so far away.' He looked at the bird. 'Can't you settle down here and be happy? You've got this beautiful tree to live in, lots of other birds for company, and you look well fed.'

Shazza lifted her wings wide, showing the soft yellow colouring underneath. Ellie thought they looked a bit like lemon meringue pie.

'Well fed!' Shazza squawked. 'Look at me. I'm feathers and bones! Besides, I'm lonely. The birds here say I'm too big and loud. I don't fit in.'

Blake frowned. 'If only we could get you onto another plane.'

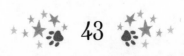

'How?' Ellie asked. 'We can't get to the airport by ourselves. And even if we could, then what?'

'She could stow away, like last time. Maybe ...'

Blake's confidence trailed off with his words. Ellie felt powerless too. It was awful to have this amazing ability to talk to animals, but not be able to use it to help one when they needed it.

'I'm sure I can fly home myself if you point me in the right direction,' Shazza said, raising herself on her claws.

'Australia's on the other side of the world, mate,' Blake said. 'Across oceans. You'd never make it.'

'Oh.' The bird's crest drooped mournfully. 'So I'm on my own then.'

Ellie wanted to give the bird a reassuring pat, but unlike Blake she was wary of Shazza's powerful beak. 'You're not on your own,' she said. 'We're here. And I'm sure that if you're nice to the other birds, they'll let you hang around with-'

Ellie didn't get to finish her sentence because Shazza suddenly gave a loud squawk. 'Look! Another aeroplane! I can hitch a ride.'

Squinting, Ellie followed the bird's gaze. She laughed. 'Shazza, that's only a drone. See how small it is?'

 45

Shazza snapped her beak scornfully. 'It looks small because it's far away.'

'It looks small because it is small. See, there's someone with a remote control.' Ellie pointed to a boy about her own age a few metres away. He was frowning with concentration as he moved the levers that made the drone fly.

Shazza was too busy screeching to listen to Ellie. 'This means I can go home! Finally!' With a flap of her powerful wings, Shazza launched herself into the air.

'No, don't!' Ellie shouted. 'You'll break it!'

Shazza ignored the warning.

 46

Chapter Four

Like an arrow shot from a crossbow, the cockatoo flew straight for the drone. With a squawk, she landed awkwardly on top of it.

'Hey, it's smaller than I am!' Shazza screeched. 'I can't get home on this!'

Blake cupped his hands around his mouth. 'Shazza, get off!' he called.

'Dad, I can't shake it off!' A man snatched the remote out of the boy's hands and fiddled frantically – uselessly – with the controls. They watched with the same expressions of horror as the drone started to drop under the cockatoo's weight.

Ellie, Blake and Choccy jogged over and joined the boy and his father.

'Sorry about that,' Blake said. 'Do you want me to try?' He held out his hand for the remote control, but the man held it out of reach.

'Is that your bird?' the man asked.

'Yeah nah,' said Blake, which Ellie had learnt meant 'no' in Australia. 'But we might be able to help.'

'Hey!' The boy pointed at the drone. 'It's going up again.'

'Stupid toy.' Shazza had gripped the drone with her claws and was flying back towards the oak tree. 'I'll teach you to trick me!'

The children raced after her, waving and shouting. Choccy barked with delight.

Blake was right, Ellie thought. Cockatoos could certainly be pests. 'Drop it, Shazza!' she called.

'Sorry, can't hear you!' Shazza said, and kept flying.

Ellie wasn't sure whether she should be talking to the bird in public, but she had to do something.

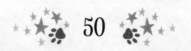

'Drop it right now or we won't help you go home!'

As suddenly as she'd grabbed it, the cockatoo let go of the drone. It spun into the oak tree and snagged on a high branch. The children skidded to a stop underneath it. Moments later the boy's father joined them, panting from the run.

He looked from the stranded drone to Ellie and Blake. 'Do you know how much that cost? Your parents will have to pay for a new one.'

Ellie paled at the thought of her mum trying to find the money for an expensive toy on top of renovating the café. 'We told you she's not ours!'

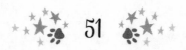

'Liar,' the boy interrupted. 'If it's not yours then how come you know it's a she and how come you know its name? You were even talking about taking it home!'

'Look,' said Blake, 'why don't I just climb up and get it for you? I'm sure it's fine.'

'No, I'll climb up and get it,' the boy said, glaring at Blake. 'You stay away.'

Not wanting to make things worse, Blake backed off.

The boy stared at the tree for a long time, as if sizing it up. Finally, he flung his arms awkwardly around the trunk. He heaved himself upwards, only to slither straight back down again. With a grunt, he tried again. The same thing happened.

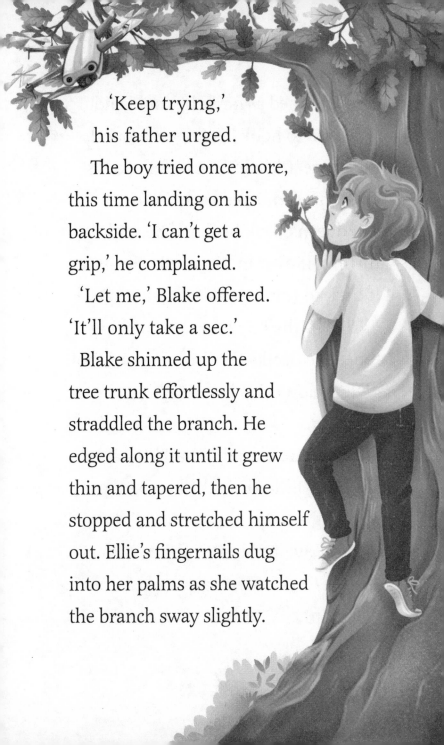

'Keep trying,'
his father urged.

The boy tried once more,
this time landing on his
backside. 'I can't get a
grip,' he complained.

'Let me,' Blake offered.
'It'll only take a sec.'

Blake shinned up the
tree trunk effortlessly and
straddled the branch. He
edged along it until it grew
thin and tapered, then he
stopped and stretched himself
out. Ellie's fingernails dug
into her palms as she watched
the branch sway slightly.

Blake reached as far as he could and managed to hook his fingers around the drone. Clasping it carefully to his chest, he clambered back down.

'It doesn't look broken,' he said, turning it over in his hands. He gave it back to the father. 'She'll be right.'

'"She"?' the boy said in a mocking tone. 'He thinks the drone's a girl too!'

'No, I don't. It's just a saying where I'm from.'

'And what planet's that?' the boy sneered. Ellie thought he was upset at being shown up by Blake, but he didn't have to be so rude.

Blake took a step backwards and fell silent.

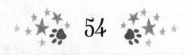

The man examined the drone carefully. After a moment he grunted. With one last dirty look at the cockatoo, he curled his arm around his son's shoulder. 'Let's go down the other end of the park.'

Shazza landed on a branch of the oak tree. By the way the bird was strutting, crest raised and head thrust forward, Ellie could tell she was still cross.

A speckled brown sparrow, tiny by comparison, fluttered onto the branch next to the cockatoo. 'I say!' the little bird scolded. 'That's not the way we do things here. People will stop feeding us if we destroy their things. Could you kindly try to remember your manners?'

Shazza cocked her head to the side. 'What did you say to me?'

The sparrow puffed up its feathers as if trying to make itself look bigger.

'If you want to fit in, stop acting like a pest. You will have to learn to behave like we do.'

'Come again?' Shazza said, creeping closer to the sparrow. 'Did you say, "snap off the

 56

branch I'm standing on"? Sounded like it to me.'

The sparrow had no time to react before Shazza chomped through the branch. It snapped in two, sending the sparrow fluttering into the air.

'Hah! Cop that!' the cockatoo squawked in delight.

'Shazza, enough!' Ellie called, but the big bird wasn't done yet. Shazza was staring at something just behind the children. Suddenly she crashed out of the tree and swooped low over their heads.

'Hey!' a voice cried.

Ellie and Blake spun around to find that two teenage girls had stopped to watch the bird and the drone. Now one

of them jumped up and snatched at
the air. Above her flapped Shazza,
with something large and rectangular
in her beak.

'Excuse me,' the girl said, clearly
flustered. 'Is that your bird? Can you
get our clipboard back?' Another
girl next to her also tried to grab the
dangling object.

'I-I'll try.' Ellie
looked up, ready to
argue with Shazza
yet again, when
the bird hurled the
clipboard at her.

Ellie ducked. Shazza cackled wildly
before perching back in the tree.

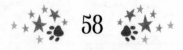

'Rotten bird,' Ellie muttered under her breath. She had bigger things to worry about than an out-of-control cockatoo – like finding out more about the new development.

'Thank you,' the teenage girl said. She bent down, picked up her clipboard and dusted it off. Turning to Ellie and Blake, she put on a big smile as if nothing out of the ordinary had happened.

'My name's Ayesha, and this is Sarah,' she said brightly. 'Would you like to sign our petition?'

Ellie knew that people made petitions when they wanted to change an unfair law or decision. If enough people

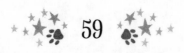

added their signatures, sometimes
they succeeded.

'What's it for?' Ellie asked.

'You like this park, right?' Ayesha
replied, waving her arms at the
surroundings. 'With all the trees
and the pond and the ... birds?'
She glanced at Shazza and clutched
her clipboard more tightly.

'Sure,' Blake said. 'Why?'

'It's being redeveloped,' Ayesha's
friend Sarah answered for her.
'Everything you see now will be buried
under concrete. There'll be nowhere
for kids to play outdoors, nowhere for
you to walk your dog, and nowhere
for the park animals to live.'

So it's true, Ellie thought. There is going to be a development here.

'No more walkies?' whimpered Choccy. 'No more play?'

And no more cat café ...

Chapter Five

'They want to build a leisure centre here,' explained Ayesha.

'It'll be huge,' Sarah chimed in. 'With a gym, tennis courts, a sports hall, fitness studios, a spa–'

'A pool?' Blake interrupted.

Ayesha nodded furiously. 'Not just a pool. A whole "aquatics centre", they're calling it. This is the biggest

green space around and there'll be nothing left of it!'

'You see that tree you're sitting under?' Sarah pointed out. 'It's hundreds of years old. It's full of birds and squirrels. Where are they going to go when it gets cut down?'

'Aairrk!' Shazza flapped her wings in a panic. 'I can't lose another home! Sign the petition! Sign it now!'

'Whoa!' Ayesha said, clapping her hands over her ears. 'Is that a cockatoo?'

'Yes,' Ellie answered. It was clear the girls couldn't understand what Shazza was saying.

'Is it yours?'

'No!' Blake was quick to say. 'It lives in the park.'

'In the wild? It must have escaped from somewhere. We should call animal rescue.' Sarah was already pulling out her phone. 'It's all right now, but I don't think it'll do well in winter.'

'That's okay,' Blake said hastily. 'My parents do animal rescues. They can sort it out.'

'Oh good! Then I'm sure they'll want you to help the other animals in the park too.' Ayesha held out the clipboard, but Blake made no move to take it.

'I'll sign,' Ellie said.

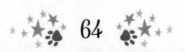

Ellie scrawled her name then held the petition out to Blake. Her new friend was scuffing the ground with his shoes.

He avoided looking at Ellie. 'Don't you want to sign it?' she prompted.

'In a sec, my shoelace is undone.' Blake crouched down to tie up his shoelace. Ellie thought he muttered something in Choccy's ear. Then the dog wagged his tail, licked Blake's chin and took off at high speed.

'Oops! I'd better catch him! See ya.' Blake ran off after the puppy without looking back.

Ellie smiled weakly at the girls. 'I'll talk to him,' she said. 'Will you be here another time?'

'Definitely,' Ayesha said. 'We need over a thousand signatures so the mayor will pay attention.'

 66

'Thanks for signing. See you around,' Sarah said.

Ellie felt a pang as she watched the girls stroll off together, side by side, heads together. Before the move, Ellie had had a friend like that. Now Marea was many miles away and the closest thing Ellie had to a friend here – or thought she had – was Blake.

'Wait up!' Ellie called after him.

Blake had crossed the park and was back at the main road waiting for the traffic lights to change. He didn't seem to hear Ellie. The second the green man flashed up, he and Choccy crossed the road

 67

and disappeared through the narrow gate at the side of their building.

The light was red again by the time Ellie reached the kerb. As she waited, she felt a puff of air near her cheek, and a weight landed on her shoulder. It was Shazza.

'Save my tree!' the cockatoo squawked in Ellie's ear. 'I need somewhere to live until I can go home.'

'I'll do my best,' Ellie promised. She expected the bird to fly back to the park. But when the lights changed and Ellie started to cross, Shazza's claws only tightened on her shoulder.

'Um, you can go back to your tree now,' Ellie said, already getting strange looks from other pedestrians. 'It's not being cut down yet.'

'I'm staying with you,' the bird said. 'I want numnums.'

'First I've got to find Blake.'

'First you've got to find food!' Shazza shouted. 'Give me something to eat or I'll bite your ear.' The bird gave a warning peck.

'Ow! All right. But keep your voice down, okay? You're going to deafen me.'

Ellie decided not to walk through the café entrance. Men were still walking in and out carrying equipment. It was best to keep out of their way, especially when she had a loud-mouthed cockatoo on her shoulder.

Ellie went through the gate to the back entrance without anyone noticing her. A few of her cats were slinking around the garden, probably avoiding all the activity in the café. They looked up at the bird, suddenly interested. Ellie rushed to the back door and closed it before the cats could follow her upstairs.

'What food have you got?' Shazza asked, bobbing her head up and down.

'Hang on a minute, let me get inside.' Ellie entered the flat and made her way to the kitchen. 'You can get off me now.'

Shazza hopped off Ellie's shoulder. She landed on the kitchen counter. Claws clicking on the smooth surface, she waddled up to a bowl of fruit. 'What are these?' she said, cocking her head sideways.

'Apples. Do you like apples?'

'I looooove apples!' Shazza squawked. 'Give me some now.'

Ellie cut off a slice and held it out to the bird. Shazza plucked it out

of her fingers and started to chomp on it. 'Blech!' she said, spitting the piece out. 'I hate apples! Apples are not numnums.'

'Okay. How about cereal?' Ellie opened the cupboard and pulled out a packet of cornflakes.

'Cereal! Yes. That's what I like. Give me cereal immediately.'

Ellie didn't fancy feeling Shazza's beak on her palm, so she spread a handful on the counter.

'Cereal, mmm,' Shazza murmured as she started munching. Then: 'Blech! I don't like cereal.' She kicked the flakes onto the floor scornfully. 'What else have you got?'

'Um ...' Ellie looked in the cupboard. 'Peanuts?'

'Hi, Ellie, hi! It's me,' a breathless voice called.

Ellie looked down and saw a small mouse crouching on the kitchen floor. She paled at how easily she might have stepped on it. Besides, the mice were supposed to stay out of sight! They had a deal.

'You shouldn't be here,' Ellie said. 'What if my mum sees you?'

'I'm Blossom,' the mouse said shyly. 'I wanted to say thank you for rescuing me.'

Ellie noticed that the mouse had a bent tail. This must be the one she'd

saved from the trap
her mum had set.

'You're welcome, but–'

'Aairrk!' Shazza
screeched. 'Lunch!' She
sailed off the counter, claws
outstretched, and gripped
Blossom with her claws.

Chapter Six

The little mouse squeaked in terror
as it rose into the air, dangling from
Shazza's claws.

'Put her down!' Ellie ordered. 'Put her
down right now!'

'I'm hungry,' Shazza said. She
perched on top of a kitchen cupboard
and held the mouse up to study it.
'Is this food?'

'No! Let her go.' Ellie felt sorry for Blossom, but she was also worried about what might happen if she got injured or – worse still – eaten. The other mice would be sure to get angry. And she wouldn't blame them!

Shazza looked at Blossom, then back at Ellie. 'It doesn't look very tasty. If I drop it, will you find my numnums?'

'I'll try! I promise.'

'All right then.' Shazza let go.

Blossom tumbled nose over tail as she plummeted towards the ground. In a flash, Ellie reached out and caught her safely. This cockatoo was proving to be a handful.

'Th-thank you, Ellie,' the mouse stuttered, raising her head. 'You saved me. Again!'

'You're welcome – again. But you've got to stay hidden from now on. Remember our deal with Herriot.'

Herriot was the grumpy caretaker mouse in charge of the building, and the first animal Ellie had been able to understand after using the magic telephone. He was so determined to guard the place until the return of someone called 'The One' that at first he had wanted to get rid of Ellie and Blake. It was only after Ellie promised to give the mice crumbs from the café that Herriot agreed to let them stay for now. In return, Ellie had asked the mice to stay out of sight of future customers – and Ellie's mum.

'I remember,' Blossom said. 'But it's good manners to say thank you when somebody helps you.'

Ellie couldn't help smiling. This mouse was very cute. 'Your name suits you,' she said.

'My dad says I'm as pretty as a flower.'

'You are.' Ellie had a sudden thought. 'Speaking of names,' she said, 'do you know anyone called Elliot?'

'No, why?'

Ellie shrugged. 'No reason.' When they met, Herriot had wondered if Ellie was Elliot. He'd seemed disappointed when she said she wasn't.

'I can find out who it is,' Blossom said, clearly determined to help. 'I can ask my brothers and sisters.'

'That'd be great, thanks. But be careful. I've thrown away all the

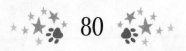 80

mouse traps, but if Mum sees you, she'll set up new ones.'

'Don't worry. I'll only come out when I'm sure you're alone.'

'Good. Oh, and here you go. Have some cereal.' Ellie picked up a scattered cornflake and offered it to the mouse.

'Fine! Feed the rat but not me,' Shazza squawked.

Ellie thought it best to ignore her.

'Thank you, Ellie!' Blossom nibbled on a cornflake. 'This is delicious.'

Ellie released the mouse gently onto the floor. 'Now off you go.'

With a twitch of her crooked tail, Blossom squeezed herself under the door and disappeared.

 81

'Now, where was I?' Ellie thought out loud. 'Oh yes, I was going to find Blake.'

'Aairrk! You said you'd give me peanuts! How will I know if they're numnums if I don't try them?'

'Later,' Ellie promised.

Thrusting her head forward, Shazza raised her crest and squawked at the top of her voice. 'Now! Keep your promise. I like peanuts. I want peanuts. Give me peanuts. You said-'

'Okay! Don't nag.' Shaking her head, Ellie opened a jar and placed a few salted nuts on the counter.

Shazza swooped on them and grasped one in her claws. She popped it in her mouth, chewed for a moment, then spat it out. 'Blech! I don't like peanuts. What else have you got?'

Ellie was starting to lose patience. 'I need to talk to Blake,' she said firmly.

'Does he have numnums?'

'Maybe. Let's go find out.'

'Let's go find out, let's go find out!' Shazza squawked, bobbing up and down.

Ellie climbed up the stairs to Blake's flat with the cockatoo perched on her shoulder. She knocked on the door and waited. There was no reply.

'He must be in there,' she said to Shazza. 'We saw him come back.'

Ellie knocked harder.

'We not home.'

Ellie recognised Choccy's voice coming from the other side of the door.

'Tell Blake to open the door!' she commanded.

'Blake not home. Me not home too.'

Ellie rolled her eyes. 'Choccy, tell Blake I want to talk to him.'

Ellie heard the scampering of claws as Choccy ran off to deliver his message. After a few moments, he was back.

'Blake no talk to you.'

Ellie stared at the closed door. Why was Blake acting like this?

She had only known him for a few days, but he'd seemed so nice and friendly. What on earth had gone wrong?

Chapter Seven

Ellie hammered on the door. She wanted to know why Blake was being so weird, and she wasn't going to give up. 'Blake! Open up!'

After what felt like a long time, Blake opened the door an inch. He spoke through the gap. 'What do you want?'

'I want to know why you didn't sign the petition,' Ellie said. Then,

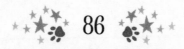

in a gentler tone, 'I want to know what's wrong. Come on, Blake, you can tell me. I'm your friend.'

Blake hesitated for a moment, then opened the door fully. 'All right. Come in.'

Ellie made her way into the living room with Shazza still perched on her shoulder. Most of the furniture was in place – a sofa, a television, two armchairs and a coffee table – but there were still unopened packing boxes all over the floor. Ellie picked her way between them and sat on the edge of a chair.

Choccy came up to her and licked her ankle. 'Sorry I lie.'

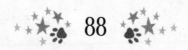

Ellie patted the
puppy on the head.
'It's not your fault.
You just did what
Blake told you to.'
She looked at Blake.

He shifted from one foot to the
other. 'I didn't want to sign the
petition straight away,' he said,
sounding defensive. 'I wanted time
to think about it.'

'What is there to think about?' Ellie
cried. 'You heard what the girls said.
The park is going to be destroyed'

'Yeah, I know.' He sat down on
the sofa and wiped a hand across
his forehead. 'But she said they're

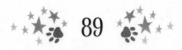

going to build a leisure centre. Think about it. We'll have a pool right across the road. We could go for a swim whenever we felt like it.'

'What about my tree?' Shazza cried. 'Save my tree!'

'Why?' Blake asked.

Ellie and Shazza stared at him, open mouthed and open beaked.

'Don't look at me like that!' Blake pushed the hair off his face. 'You don't even like living in that tree. You said so yourself. You said you don't fit in with the other birds.'

Shazza raised her crest and looked like she was about to argue, but Ellie raised a hand for silence. The bird jumped off her shoulder and landed on the coffee table.

'Go on,' Ellie said, her eyes fixed on Blake's face.

'It's just ... Shazza's not the only one who misses Australia. You don't know what it's like,' Blake said, staring at his feet, 'always moving from one house to another. We haven't stayed anywhere for more than two years. Whenever I make friends, I just go and lose them again.'

As if sensing his master's sadness, Choccy pressed himself against Blake's legs.

'But, however many times we moved in the past, at least we

stayed in the same country. Now I'm on the other side of the world!' Blake said. 'It's different here. I miss my old life. I miss going for a swim at the beach every day.'

Ellie spoke slowly. 'So ... you think going to a pool would make you less homesick?'

'I don't know. Yes. Maybe.' Blake shook his head. 'I just wanted time to think about it.'

'I thought you liked it here. When we met, you seemed so happy, so friendly.'

'Yeah, well, I have to try, don't I? But I'd rather be home, in a place I know and where I don't have to try. I ... I'm

not sure I'll fit in here.' Blake hung
his head as if embarrassed.

'Yes, you will!' Ellie said. 'You're
nice. I'm the one who'll have trouble.
I'm-' she shrugged. 'I don't make
friends easily.'

'At least you're in your own country.
Sometimes it's like I don't even speak
the same language!'

'But I'm not in my hometown. This
place is new to me, too. I miss my
old friends and I don't know if I can
make new ones. I've never had to
try before.'

Ellie and Blake stared at each other
in silence. They both looked surprised
to realise that they had more in

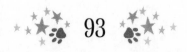

common than their new home and
ability to understand animals.

Choccy moved away from Blake
to press himself against Ellie's
legs. 'I your new friend,' he said.
Touched, Ellie leant down and
ruffled the dog's fur.

'And so am I,' Blake said.

'Yeah?' Ellie said. 'But you won't sign
a petition to save my mum's café?'

Blake's cheeks flushed red. 'When
you put it that way ...'

'This is getting us nowhere,' Shazza
said, waddling along the coffee table.
'Talk, talk, talk! You're forgetting the
most important thing here.'

'Your tree?' Ellie asked.

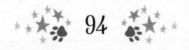

'My numnums!'
She fluttered up
and perched on
top of Blake's head.
'What have you got to eat?'

Chapter Eight

'Hey, that hurts!' Blake swatted at the cockatoo perched on his head.

'I'll hop off when you give me some food,' Shazza said, and pecked at Blake's ear.

'Ow! Get off, or you'll get nothing,' Blake scolded.

Shazza leapt onto Blake's shoulder, making him look a bit like a pirate

with an over-sized parrot.

'Right. Let's go,' the cockatoo said
and fluttered her wings.

Blake didn't object to Shazza
riding his shoulder as they strolled
into the kitchen. 'How about some
chips?' he said, opening a cupboard
door.

'You can make chips?' Ellie asked,
her eyebrows shooting to the top
of her head. 'Can I have some?'

'Make them? They're ready-made.'

Ellie watched as Blake dug out a
colourful plastic packet and held
it up.

'Oh. You mean crisps,' she said.

'Chips.'

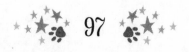 97

Ellie was confused. 'If they're chips, then what do you call the things you eat with fish?'

'Also chips. Or maybe hot chips, if you wanna be fussy.'

'I'm not eating that!' Shazza squawked, snapping her beak. 'Get it away from me!'

'She got her head stuck in an empty crisp packet,' Ellie explained, seeing Blake's baffled expression. 'Anyway: chips, crisps, it doesn't matter what you call them. It's the same thing.' She didn't want to make her new friend feel even more out of place.

Blake grinned. 'You say *tomayto*, I say *tomahto*.'

'Tomato?' Shazza echoed. 'Tomato is definitely food! Give me some.'

'We don't have any,' Blake closed the cupboard. He looked at his puppy, who was nosing around on the floor. 'I know, we can try Choccy's biscuits.'

'Huh?' Choccy looked up. 'Bickie for me?'

'For you.' Blake handed Choccy a treat, and then held one out for the cockatoo. 'And for you.'

Shazza snatched the biscuit out of Blake's hand with her sharp beak. She moved it to one foot and eyed it warily. 'Is this bird food?'

'No,' said Blake.

'Good. I hate bird food.' Shazza took

a big bite out of the dog biscuit and spat it out. 'Blech! Horrible. It tastes like dirt. Choccy's one looks better.'

Shazza dropped down to the floor and waddled towards the dog. Alarmed, Choccy picked his biscuit up in his jaws and darted into the living room. Squawking, the bird hurried after him.

'Come back or I'll chomp on your tail! You know I'll do it!'

Ellie and Blake threw back their heads and laughed.

'You know, Shazza actually makes me feel less homesick,' Blake said, finally catching his breath. 'How can I miss Australia when there's a piece of it over here with me?'

'As long as you don't try bringing any spiders or snakes over.' Ellie shuddered. She knew Australia was home to some of the most venomous animals in the world, and she wasn't keen to meet any of them.

Blake chuckled. 'I'll try not to. But I did bring something else ...'

Ellie watched as Blake went to the fridge and pulled out bread and butter.

'All this talk of food made me hungry,' Blake said. 'How would you like to try an Australian delicacy?'

Ellie pulled out a stool and sat at the kitchen counter. She looked at the ingredients. 'I hate to tell you this, but we have sandwiches here too.'

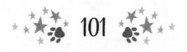

'Not like this. First you need a good thick spread of butter,' Blake said, matching his actions to his words.

'A butter sandwich?'

'Wait.'

Ignoring the crashing, squawking and scampering sounds coming from the living room, Blake took a jar out of a cupboard. It was small and black, with a red and yellow label. Ellie squinted at it.

'What's that?'

'Vegemite. Ever tried it?' Blake removed the lid. Inside was a thick, dark paste.

'Well, no,' Ellie confessed. 'But it looks like Marmite, and that's awful.'

'The mistake most people make,' Blake said, dipping the tip of a knife in the jar, 'is they spread it on too thick. All you need is a thin smear.' He prepared the sandwich, sliced it and gave half to Ellie. 'Go on, try it.'

Elie raised the sandwich halfway to her mouth, then stopped. 'Only if you promise to sign the petition.'

'Hey, that's not fair!' But Blake was grinning. 'Okay, you win. I guess I was being selfish. I don't want your mum's business to flop. I'll sign the petition – so eat up.'

Ellie took a cautious sniff of the sandwich.

'It's, uh, quite a strong smell ...'

'NUMNUMS!'

Before Ellie could take a bite, Shazza
shot in from the living room and
snatched the sandwich with her claws.

She broke off a big chunk and gobbled
it up.

'Finally!' the bird screeched,
waggling her head back and forth in
ecstasy. 'I've found my numnums!'

Chapter Nine

'So that's what numnums are!' Ellie said, clapping her hands with delight. 'You like Vegemite sandwiches. That's what your owner – I mean your human – used to feed you.'

Shazza was too busy eating to reply.

'No wonder she was unhappy,' Blake said through a mouthful of his own sandwich. 'You can't find these

in the wild.' He looked at
Ellie's empty hand.
'Oops, sorry,
I should have
offered you mine.

Want me to make you another?'

'No thanks, I'm not very hungry,'
Ellie lied, wrinkling her nose.

'Another, another!' Shazza
squawked, pecking at the jar.

'Oi, keep your big beak out of it.'
Blake jerked the precious Vegemite
away and set to work making
another sandwich.

'I can live here with you!' Shazza
said. 'You can be my friends and
give me numnums every day.'

Blake shook his head violently.
'No way! My parents would go nuts.
I had enough trouble convincing
them to let me have Choccy.'

'How about she stays in her tree?'
Ellie suggested. 'We can visit her
when we take Choccy for walks, and
we can take her some sandwiches.'

'Sure,' Blake said, reluctantly giving
Shazza half of the second sandwich.
'Let's take her back now.'

They tried to keep out of sight
by going out the back way again,
but Ellie's mum stopped them on
the footpath. Her bracelets tinkled
merrily as she waved.

'Kids, come and see!' she called.

'The workmen have gone, and we're all–' She stopped when she saw Shazza. 'Where did that come from?'

'We found her in the park,' Ellie answered truthfully. 'She must be an escaped pet.'

'The poor thing! Maybe your parents can help find its home, Blake?'

Blake nodded.

'Just don't bring it inside,' Ellie's mum went on. 'I don't want it making a mess – or stirring up the cats. There's an old birdcage in the back garden. You can put it in that for now.'

'Aairrk!' Shazza squawked. 'No cage!'

109

'Fly back to your tree,' Blake told Shazza in a low voice, so as not to be overheard. 'I promise I'll bring you more numnums later.' With another squawk and a flap of her wings, the large bird soared across the road and into the park.

Ellie's mum watched Shazza fly away. 'Never mind. If you see it again, try to rescue it. But for now ...' she stepped aside theatrically. 'Welcome to Cattucino!'

Ellie and Blake walked through the café's entrance, and Ellie caught her breath. The change was astonishing. The once gloomy space was now bright and inviting. There was a broad countertop ready to display delicious cakes, as well as a shiny new espresso maker with knobs, spouts and buttons everywhere. Tables and chairs were arranged neatly in one part of the room, while the other side had cosy armchairs and rugs.

'People can choose where they'd like to sit,' Ellie's mum explained. 'I wanted it to look really homey.'

Scratching posts and cat baskets dotted the floor. Now that the workmen had left, some of the cats had already made their way to their new beds. Mozart, the oldest cat and Ellie's favourite, was curled up,

snoring softly. Ellie checked that
Choccy stayed obediently by
Blake's side.

'Good boy,' she murmured softly, just as Blake said the same. They grinned at each other.

'See those perches?' Ellie's mum continued. She pointed to some small shelves mounted on the walls. They were placed at different heights and looked like the rungs of a ladder climbing up the wall. 'They give the cats somewhere to go when they've had enough of being fussed over. They can also escape through there.' She showed them a cat flap in the door that led to the storage room.

'You need calm and happy cats to run a cat café!'

'This looks great, Mum,' Ellie said, and she meant it. She'd never expected the café to look so good. She breathed a sigh of relief. Maybe Mum was right when she said they'd be a success despite the development across the road.

'Now there's only one thing left to do,' Mum said. 'I thought you might like to help me with it.'

'We'd love to, Mrs Walsh,' Blake said. 'What would you like us to do?'

'See those old papers on the windows?' Ellie's mum pointed to the yellowing newspapers

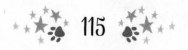 115

that covered the building's front windows. 'Rip them off and show the world we're ready for business!'

Ellie and Blake tugged enthusiastically at the papers. They were so old and dried out that some crumbled between their fingers. Choccy pounced on the scraps as they fell to the floor. More than once, Blake had to pull chewed up bits of paper out of the dog's mouth.

'These must have been up for years,' Blake said, wrestling another soggy wad from the puppy.

'Yeah. It's kind of fun seeing the place open up at last.' Ellie ripped off a piece of newspaper and dropped

it at her feet. She happened to look down as it settled.

'Hey. What's this?' Ellie said, bending down to scoop it up. She examined it closely and gasped.

Blake stood, wiping his hands on his jeans. 'What?' he said, coming to look over her shoulder. He read the headline aloud: '"Local vet committed to" - something. Where's the rest of it?' When Ellie still didn't answer him, he followed her gaze to an old photo.

Like the headline it was torn, but it showed a man with an untidy beard and intense eyes. 'Do you recognise him?' Blake asked.

Ellie managed a nod.

'It's my great-grandfather.'

Robbie the Rebel Squirrel

Ellie is desperately searching for answers about what happened to her *great-grandfather* years ago. But when she and Blake get caught up in the middle of an *animal war* in the local park, there are more pressing things to think about.

Robbie the *red squirrel* and his clan are clashing with the bigger, meaner grey squirrels. As Robbie bravely stands up to the *Greys*, Ellie and Blake do their best to stop the squirrels from fighting and bring *peace* to the park.

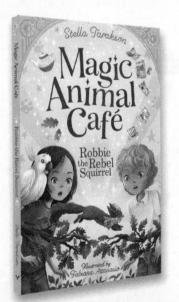

Read on for a sneak peak at
at the next book in the series!

Magic Animal Café

Robbie
the Rebel
Squirrel

Stella Tarakson

Illustrated by
Fabiana Attanasio

Sweet
Cherry

Chapter One

Ellie stared at the torn piece of newspaper in her hands and gasped.

'What?' Blake asked, stopping what he was doing.

Ellie and Blake had been tearing off the papers that covered the old building's windows. The papers had been there for many years. Now that the building was ready

to become a new cat café, it was time to let in some light and show it off to the world.

Blake looked over her shoulder. He read the headline out loud: '"Local vet committed to" – something. Where's the rest of it?'

Ellie didn't answer.

'Do you recognise him?' Blake asked.

Ellie managed a nod. 'It's my great-grandfather.'

'He was in the paper? How come?'

'I don't know.' Ellie stared at the photo of a man with messy hair, an untidy beard and intense eyes. 'He used to own this building. He left it

to Mum when he died a few years
ago. I never met him, but Mum
once showed me photos of him.
He looked different, but he was
a vet, just like this says. It must
be him.'

'Is he the one who had a few –'
Blake tapped the side of his head
'–problems?'

'Yeah.' Ellie still hadn't taken
her eyes off the photo. Her great-
grandfather hadn't
looked so messy
in the ones
Mum had
shown her.
In those,

he had slicked back hair and a neatly trimmed beard. His eyes had shone with happiness. Ellie wondered what happened to change him.

'So, what's the story with him?'

Ellie shrugged. 'Mum never said.'

'You can ask her now,' Blake pointed out.

'I could, but Mum doesn't like talking about him. She was pretty upset when he died.'

After a moment, Blake asked: 'What does "committed" mean?'

'I'm not sure what it means here,' Ellie admitted, looking at the paper again. 'This says "committed to" ... and the rest is gone.'

'It was his phone, wasn't it?'
Blake asked. 'The magic one?'

When Ellie first moved into the
building, she'd found a mysterious
old trunk locked away in a
cupboard. Inside the trunk was
an old-fashioned black telephone.
After dialling a number written
on it, Ellie and Blake were both
stunned and delighted to discover
that they were able to talk to
animals. For the first time, Ellie
wondered whether her great-
grandfather had been able to do
that too. Maybe he was the one
who wrote the numbers on the
dial!

Suddenly, Ellie was seized with a need to find out more about her great-grandfather.

'Where's the rest of this article? Let's check the floor ...'